a min**e**dition book

published by Michael Neugebauer Publishing Ltd HK

Text copyright © 2009 by Tatiana and Rafael Bellavita
Illustrations copyright © 2009 by Feeroozeh Golmohammadi
Originally published by Michael Neugebauer Publishing Ltd., Hong Kong.
Rights arranged with "minedition" Rights and Licensing AG, Zurich, Switzerland.
Published simultaneously in Canada.
Manufactured in China
Typesetting in Optima
Color separation by Hi Fai

Library of Congress Cataloging-in-Publication Data available upon request.

ISBN 978-988-97794-6-7

10 9 8 7 6 5 4 3 2 1
First Impression

For more information please visit our website: www.minedition.com, or: www.maiadreams.com

MAIA DREAMS
STAR RUBY

by Tatiana & Rafael Bellavita

with Pictures by Feeroozeh Golmohammadi

minedition

Magically, a beautiful Golden Eagle
appears at Maia's window and says,
"Come and fly with me to a far away place."

Maia and Baron crawl onto the Golden Eagle's
back and he says, "My name is Golden Shine"...

and they fly away into the beautiful night sky
with the stars and the moon lighting their way.

"Where are you taking us?" Maia asks.

"We are going to a beautiful land where the giant elephants and tigers roam. It is a land where people live together in harmony with these noble animals," Golden Shine replies.

Maia is happy to hear of such a place.

As they fly through the star-lit sky, the night turns slowly into day. Below they see enchanting palaces and people riding amazing giant white elephants.

Golden Shine glides
down and lands beneath
a great big white elephant.
"Hello," says the elephant, "my name
is Jaingbu. Welcome!"

Maia, Baron and Golden Shine greet
the giant with friendly smiles.

Jaingbu has lived here for a very long
time, and the people love and respect
him.
"There is much to see in our land,
and we have many treasures,"
he tells them. "The Star Ruby is
one. It is a stone formed in our
land and is very special."

"How is it special?" asks Maia.

Jaingbu tells them, "Many believe when they feel sadness,
if they put a star ruby near their heart
they will begin to feel happy again."

"I have heard such stories in the other lands I have visited,"
Golden Shine says with excitement.

"Yes, and we have many other wonderful stones,"
Jiangbu continues.

Maia and Baron listen with great attention but then something distracts them.

Baron begins to bark!
He hears a rustling sound and then a roar
and sees something behind a tree!

"It is a Bengal Tiger!" says Jaingbu,
"and she is my friend."
"Greetings," says the tiger, "and welcome!
I am Darika."

Maia begins to giggle and Baron barks.
Darika has something stuck behind her ear.
"Why are you laughing?" asks Darika.
Maia gently removes a heart
shaped leaf.

"You had this leaf stuck behind
your ear."

Jaingbu says to them, "That is
a leaf from the beautiful
Bodhi Tree. It is a sacred tree
and is honored and loved
throughout the land.

Something catches Maia's eye—a beautiful shining light.
Maia, Golden Shine and Baron walk and walk until they see the big rock
where the light is coming from.
As they get closer they see that there are stones within the rock.
These stones shine with an amazing red splendor!

"Could this be what Jaingbu spoke of?" asks Maia.

Then the red stone begins to speak...

They look in amazement.
"Who are you?" asks Maia.

"I am Star Ruby and it was here I was born."

"How is a stone born?" asks Maia.

Star Ruby answers, "When a volcano erupted many years ago,
I was mixed with air, water and many other minerals. With time,
I became hard and red like I am now.
Many people like to wear a star ruby on their clothes
or near their heart as a symbol of love."

"We have only begun to see this wonderful land," says Golden Shine to
Maia and Baron, "but it is time, and we must fly."

Star Ruby calls out to Maia,
"If you take me with you, I will shine upon your days and nights
so you will always remember this land."

"Oh, thank you." Maia says and holds the stone tightly in her hand. "I will
treasure you always and keep you near my heart and will never forget
the lovely land where you were born."

They find Jiangbu, the friendly elephant and Darika, the beautiful tiger. They thank them for their kindness and for telling them about Star Ruby and the Bodhi Tree.

Golden Shine spreads his wings with Maia and Baron on his shoulders. They fly up into the beautiful blue sky which then turns into night.

Suddenly Maia hears
her mother's gentle whisper,
"It is time to wake up."
Maia sits up on her bed half
asleep and realizes it was
a dream.
It had all seemed so real!

But when Maia opens her
hand she sees the beautiful
red stone.

"Baron, it's Star Ruby!" she
says with delight...

...and Baron barks with
excitement!!!